ELEANOR'S DILEMMA

Cheryl Wright

Table of Contents

ELEANOR'S DILEMMA

Copyright © 2019 Cheryl Wright

Small Town Romance Publications

ALL RIGHTS RESERVED

Dedication

To Margaret Tanner, my very dear friend and fellow author, for her enduring encouragement and friendship.

To Alan, my husband of over forty-six years, who has been a relentless supporter of my writing and dreams for many years.

To You, my wonderful readers, who encourage me to continue writing these stories. It is such a joy knowing so many of you enjoy reading my stories as much as I love writing them for you.

Prologue

Great Falls, Nebraska

1881

Eleanor Carter was not long awake and making up the bed when she heard ear-piercing screams coming from the sitting room.

Momentarily she froze.

Shaking with fear, she silently went to the bedroom door and opened it a fraction. What she saw left her horrified. Two men, both with guns and daggers, were attacking her dear husband, Nathaniel.

"Where's the money?" one man yelled, plunging a knife into Nathaniel's stomach.

She covered her mouth with both hands to stop herself from screaming.

What should she do? Could she get help in time?

She'd lived a privileged life, there was no doubt about it, and this house, or mansion as some preferred to call it, had plenty of places to hide. But she was certain these animals wouldn't want to leave any witnesses behind.

"There's no money in the house," she heard Nathaniel say, his voice wavering. The knife plunged into his stomach again.

"You fool," the other man shouted moments later. "That's not helping. You've gone and killed him." He covered his face with his hands. "What are we going to do now?"

She swallowed hard as she watched the life drain out of her husband, then did the only thing she could think to do. Escape.

Eleanor quietly opened the bedroom window, slipping out onto the wet, dew-covered grass. Although it was late May, the air was still crisp, and often chilly this time of the morning.

So early in fact, she hadn't yet put on her boots, and the ground beneath her feet was cold and damp. As her bare feet hit the ground, she stopped, listening for any indication they knew she was even in the house.

The wind whistling through the now open window pushed on the slightly open door, and it creaked. Eleanor cringed.

"What was that?"

She knew what would happen if they found her, so she ran. She didn't look back until she was safely huddled in a small cave not far from the falls that fell on their property.

Even then she didn't allow herself to cry for her dear husband, Nathanial. What if they heard? For they would surely be out looking for her. Listening for any indication she was there.

Her heart was hollow – her Nathaniel was dead. She tried not to think about the torture he'd endured, but it would surely insinuate itself into her nightmares for many years to come.

She grieved for her husband, and grieved for the life they'd planned. They wanted a family together, at least four children, and now that would never happen. She fought back a sob, fearing for her life.

Eleanor stopped. She could hear voices in the distance and decided it was no longer safe in the small cave. She carefully edged to the opening, and with no one in sight, slid out and ran to the nearby falls, silently slipping in behind them.

It was a secret place that only she and Nathaniel knew about. They would often go to the river in the heat of summer and swim there.

She recalled the first time they were swimming and Nathaniel disappeared. She was panic stricken believing him drowned, but he was hiding behind the falls, and was totally invisible.

He hid for what seemed an eternity, and she was near hysterical before he showed himself. She never forgave him for terrifying her that day.

Now she was grateful because it may be what saves her life.

Chapter One

Willowbridge, Montana

1881

Eleanor Carter stared out the window of the stagecoach.

This was not where she wanted to be. Willowbridge, Montana was not on her wish list, never had been. She preferred the hustle and bustle of *Great Falls, Nebraska.*

Her favorite pastime was shopping – for gowns, and for boots especially. She loved to socialize, to get out amongst the richest of the rich.

She attended high society balls at least once a month. Nathaniel didn't care much for them, but he cared for her, loved her, and went along with her because it made her happy. It also helped his standing in the community.

She fervently wished she was back home, but it wasn't to be. Couldn't be.

She pulled her thoughts from the tragedy that had recently occurred and absorbed the countryside. It reminded her so much of her beloved Nebraska, especially this time of year.

The fragrance of nature assailing her senses was a welcomed memory.

Normally she would love the scene before her – undulating mountains with massive trees clumped close together, wild flowers scattered about, and long green grass. Birds twittering reminded her so much of home. Of their home – out in the middle of nowhere, and away from everything else.

It also reminded her of the day she had no choice but to trample through the dew-covered grass, in her feet bare running for her life.

She swallowed back a sob.

The stagecoach slowed, and she turned her attention to the town of Willowbridge, now visible, and grimaced.

"What are you thinking?"

She glanced at Glen Sanders sitting opposite, then ran her hands down her skirts. She felt far from presentable.

She lifted her head momentarily before answering. "What a miserable one-horse town

I've been dragged into." She almost spat the words out.

He glared at her. "This one-horse town as you call it," he said between gritted teeth, "will likely save your life."

He was right, she knew he was, but that didn't mean she had to be happy about it.

She just hoped the ranch he had organized and she paid for, was livable. Eleanor knew it was wishful thinking but what choice did she have?

Glen, gentleman he was, helped her down from the stagecoach.

"Thank you," she said. Despite her current demeanor, her manners were inbuilt.

Their eyes met.

"You are welcome, darling," he said, glancing at Jackson Hillside, the stagecoach driver, hovering nearby.

"I have some errands to attend to," he told Jackson. "Is there somewhere my wife can wait with our luggage until I return?"

They were directed to a small cafe not far away. "You can wait there at the Willowbridge Café. Get a bit to eat too, if you want."

He thanked the man and led his wife to the café, where he deposited her and their luggage.

"Welcome!" The smiling waitress hovered next to her, waiting for her order. "I'm Cherry, and I'll be looking after you."

Eleanor forced herself to smile. It wasn't Cherry's fault she was in a foul mood because she didn't want to be here in Willowbridge.

"What would you like?"

Eleanor glanced through the menu. "Thank you, Cherry," she said amicably. "I'll have a black tea with a slice of lemon, and..." she perused the snacks. "I would love a biscuit with jam." She looked up and smiled at the young woman.

"I'll be right back."

Eleanor settled in her seat, then watched as her *husband* accosted the sheriff as he did his rounds. After a heated discussion, the two men headed in the opposite direction.

As she sipped her tea, Eleanor wondered how much Glen Sanders would tell the sheriff about her sinister predicament.

Glen slumped down in the chair and ordered a coffee. "Strong and black. And I'll have one of those too, thanks" he said to Cherry, pointing at Eleanor's biscuit with jam.

"I gather it didn't go well," she said, noticing the miserable look on his face.

He shook his head. "Sheriff Black was none to happy I'd not let him know in advance we were coming. But as I explained to him, we couldn't risk word getting out."

He lowered his voice as Cherry returned with his order. "Can you point me to the Mercantile," he asked as she was about to leave.

"Cross Main Street, then it's a few doors up."

"Really? Do we have to?" Eleanor said, annoyed.

Cherry laughed. "You don't like shopping?" She obviously thought it a joke. But to Eleanor it wasn't.

"My, uh, wife is a bit of a recluse," Glen explained, hoping that would cover them for their lack of appearance in the future. It was sure to be noticed in a town this small. He'd already told her it was going to be tricky to explain their lack of participation in a place of this size.

They didn't even know it existed until one of his former colleagues from the Pinkerton Detectives said he had a cousin five times removed living there. They hadn't seen each other in decades due to its remote location.

It would be the perfect hideaway until the law was able to find the men who murdered Eleanor's husband.

Glen stood as he gulped down the last mouthful of his coffee. "If you're ready, we'll go," he said, then turned to Cherry. "Could we leave our luggage here while we run a few errands? I don't mind paying."

Of course he didn't. It wasn't his money. Despite her inward annoyance, she smiled at the waitress who complied with the request, but pushed the notes aside. "Our pleasure," she said, guiding Glen to the place he could leave their few measly belongings.

At least *he* had spare clothes and a few personal items; she had nothing. Glen told her they couldn't risk going back to the house in case she was seen. Eleanor knew he was right.

She'd hidden behind those falls for what seemed a lifetime, but was in fact three days. She figured the killers would have given up by then, and she was right. Still, it had been a risk to ride into town for help.

Her mind swung back to the present when Glen led her outside and they headed to the Mercantile.

The sun was shining, and the sky was blue. If Eleanor hadn't known better, she'd think it was a glorious day. She took the opportunity to look around the Main Street. It wasn't Great Falls, but at least she would be able to pick up some supplies here.

As they entered the Mercantile, they were warmly welcomed. "Welcome, welcome," Livvy Holland said, before introducing herself. "This is my husband, Harry, and I'm Livvy. You're new in town!"

She sounded so excited to see them, and under any other circumstances, Eleanor would be too. She loved to socialize, but not on this level so much.

Glen extended his hand to Harry Holland. "I'm Glen Sanders, and this is my wife, Eleanor."

Livvy stepped forward and hugged her warmly. "It's so nice to meet you."

Eleanor sank into her. She fought back the tears that stung her eyes, but couldn't let them free. Her arms went up around the other woman, and she held tight. She knew that under other circumstances they could be friends.

Of course Livvy wasn't on her level in society, but that wouldn't stop them being friends. Not in a place like this, anyway.

She let her arms fall to her sides. "I need some supplies please," she said, mustering up the best smile she could. "Gowns and other, er, personal items."

Glen intervened. "Her luggage was lost on our trip here," he explained. How he came up with these stories on the fly, she'd never know.

Livvy escorted her to the gowns, bonnets, undergarments and other personal items she would need. "We'll open an account for you," she said cordially.

Glen glanced across to where they stood. "No need. We'll pay in cash." Harry stared at him. "We won't be around much. My wife is a bit of a recluse," he said, using the same explanation as before. At least his story was consistent.

Once she'd made all her purchases, they loaded up with food and other supplies such as blankets and pillows. Traveling light did have its drawbacks.

"If you can hold onto these until I get the wagon?" Wagon? She had no knowledge of a wagon. "I hired one from the livery. We need to get to the ranch, and I knew we'd have supplies, darling." He grinned at her, and she wanted to slap him. He pulled her close to his side.

He was going just a little too far with this façade. If they hadn't been in public, she would have slapped his face.

"That's fine," Harry said. "Where are you going to live, if you don't mind me asking?"

Her heart raced. It was probably an innocent enough question, but would it put them in danger?

"We bought an old ranch about ten miles south east of Willowbridge. Got it for a bargain – the Land Agent said it was all but abandoned."

"I think I know where you mean. The old Jones place. Heck, that's been empty for a couple of years, since the old man died." He scratched his head. "I hate to think what you might find out there."

"Hopefully it's not too bad. If it is, we'll stay at the hotel for a few days until I can fix it."

Harry scratched his head again. "We can probably get a bunch of fellows out there to help. That's what we do around here."

Panic hit her in the chest, and she felt Glen's arm creep up her back, and hold her tight again. His reassurance helped calm her racing heart.

"Thanks for the offer, but I don't want to put anyone out. I'll check it out first. It might be fine."

"Have it your way," Harry said, a puzzled look on his face. Then he smiled. "You're city folks, aren't you," he said, brightening up.

Glen laughed. "Does it show that much?" Then they left to collect the wagon from the livery.

Their innocent trip to the Mercantile had been one of terror for the new widow.

Chapter Two

Eleanor groaned as they pulled up outside the ranch. Her ranch.

It appeared old and rundown. A few palings had fallen off, and the roof needed repairs as well.

Glen helped her down from the wagon, and she opened the gate. It fell off in her hands.

This was far from what she was used to. With her husband being the pillar of society back in Great Falls, they had the largest house on the biggest block of land.

Nathaniel had built the six-bedroom mansion with their future family in mind. It included a study where he could work at home, and a classroom where their children could be homeschooled.

She stood with the remnants of the wooden gate in her hands, tears rolling down her face. She hadn't heard him come up behind her, and was startled as Glen took the gate out of her hands.

"It will be alright," he said gently.

She stared at him as she swiped at her cheeks. "You don't know that," she spat. She took a deep breath. "I hope the interior isn't as bad as the outside."

He pulled the keys from his pocket and unlocked the door. Eleanor gazed through the windows. It wasn't home, but it would have to do. She had no other choice.

Glen stepped inside. "It looks cozy. The furniture is covered with sheets, so at least it won't be dusty."

He was right, but what was underneath? She pulled off the sheet covering the sofa. It was surprisingly pretty. She pushed at it with her fingers – it felt solid, good quality. And it was large.

She eyed her *husband*. It might even be large enough for him to sleep on, despite his height.

Eleanor wandered around the room. It needed a good dusting and a sweep, but it wasn't too bad considering it had been locked up for a couple of years. The fireplace needed cleaning out, and the windows needed a wash, but she could manage.

It wasn't unlike her childhood home. She swallowed back emotion as she thought of her sister, Cassandra, who had no idea where she was, or that Nathaniel was dead.

She swiped at her cheek again, and turned away from Glen, moving into the kitchen. It looked out over the rest of the property, which was said to be over a hundred acres.

It was a pretty area, she couldn't deny that, and those rolling hills in the distance reminded her of home. She and Nathaniel would often sit out back at sunrise and enjoy a hot coffee before he had to leave for work.

She sniffled, pulling her thoughts away from the past, and looked about the kitchen. It was quite large compared to the rest of the house, but she understood the reason.

The Land Agent had said it was a booming horse property in its day, and employed several farmhands and cowboys. As part of their cover, Glen wanted to bring it back up to that level.

She didn't care either way – her finances allowed her to do it, and if it helped keep her safe, why not? She would end up selling it when all this was over, so it didn't matter to her.

She opened the door to the wood stove. It needed a good clean, just like the fireplace. When the owner died, it seemed the place had just been closed up, never to be used again.

Upon opening the cupboards, Eleanor discovered she had a well-equipped kitchen to work with. She loved to cook, so that was at least one thing in its favor.

The pantry was, not surprisingly, in need of a good clean. Everything would have to go. It might mean another trip into town, but she hoped not. The less she was seen, the better.

Glen had drummed that into her from the moment he'd taken on her protection detail. The sheriff at Great Falls was investigating, but didn't hold out much hope of finding her husband's killers. He'd put it down to a robbery gone wrong. And from what she'd seen, that was true.

Their faces were etched in her mind, which had helped a lot with building a sketch for circulation to law enforcement. Hence the reason she had to go into hiding.

She was pulled out of her thoughts at the sound of movement behind her, and she gasped.

"It's just me," Glen said gently, as he put their supplies on the counter. "Where do you want these?"

She relaxed just hearing his voice. "I, I have to clean the pantry first. Leave them there for now." She turned and stared at the tranquility out the back window again. The peacefulness of the place made her feel more relaxed, calm.

Unlocking the back door, Eleanor stepped outside. The sun hit her in the face and she was momentarily blinded. She closed her eyes and absorbed the warmth of the day before venturing further.

"Oh, there's a chicken coop," she called to Glen. He joined her outside. "I had chickens as a child. My sister and I had to collect the eggs every day. We even named each chicken, and cried when one died." She swallowed back her emotion. She'd never felt so devastated – would she ever see Cassandra again?

"We could probably get some chickens, if that's what you want. I'll make enquiries."

She nodded. "I'd like that." It was such a small gesture, but it made her happy. For the moment anyway.

"There's a horse ranch not far from Willowbridge, the Johannson Ranch. We'll go there tomorrow and buy our first round of horses."

She looked to the barn. "I wonder what state it's in."

Their footsteps echoed as they stepped inside the huge building. It was bigger than the house itself, and reminded Eleanor so much of her childhood. Not the size, because theirs was far from large, but the smell. The odor that told her horses had lived here.

She wondered if her memories would leave her alone anytime soon, or if she was destined to recall every past moment while living on this ranch.

She truly hoped not, because it was playing havoc with her heart.

Glen shuffled behind her, and she turned to see him enter the tack room, which was well-equipped. At least she wouldn't have to invest in saddles and other necessary items. It was all here. "I feel like we're stepping into someone else's life," she said softly. "He must have died suddenly. So much of his life has been left behind."

It reminded her of her own life. She couldn't return to the house after the killers had left. Couldn't bear to see Nathaniel like that. Instead she'd hidden for days, then when it was safe, rode frantically into town, going directly to the sheriff's office.

She would never return to the home she and Nathaniel had shared. There were far too many awful memories in that house now; they completely overtook the good ones.

Besides, it was already on the market. The money from the sale of it would be deposited in her bank account, which she would likely need down the track.

"Before we do anything else, the wood stove needs to be started. No stove, no coffee," she said, knowing that would stir him up. In the short time she'd known Glen, she'd already come to understand he enjoyed his coffee. If there was one thing he couldn't do without, that was it.

They headed back toward the house. "That must be the wood shed," he said, pointing to a small box on the side of the house. Let's hope it's not empty."

She left him to check while she explored the remaining rooms. In particular, the bedroom.

Eleanor stood in the doorway, and glanced around the large room. Like the rest of the house, the bed was covered with a large sheet. It had been stripped bare, and she hoped there was linen somewhere in the house. It was one of the few things she hadn't considered.

She opened one door of the wardrobe that ran along an entire wall, and found a neat pile of sheets, towels, and blankets. She crinkled her nose at the musty smell, and left the door open to air out. She also opened a window – that might help too.

There were two more doors to the wardrobe, and she opened them. Both were hanging space. The first stood empty, so she presumed the wife had died before Mr Jones, and her things had been cleared out. She moved to the next door, and swallowed. What would she find here?

Just as she'd feared, men's clothing hung in the cupboard. There was a handful of shirts, some pants, plus an almost pristine suit, for church no doubt. They were far too small for Glen, so she pulled them all out and threw them roughly on the unmade bed.

When they were next in Willowbridge, she'd donate them to the church. Someone might as well get the use from them.

Her mother's voice echoed in her head. She'd not grown up privileged, nor had they been poor. When the girls outgrew their clothes and shoes, provided they were still in good condition, they were donated to the church. Nothing of use was ever thrown away.

She carefully folded each item, and put them aside on the easy chair sitting in the corner.

Glen cleared his throat behind her. "What's all this?"

She stared at him. "Mr Jones clothes I'm guessing. We can take them to the church when we're next in town."

He put up a hand as if to stop her. "I *will* be going to church," she said adamantly. "No one knows us here, so it will be safe." She ignored his protests and continued folding. There would be no argument.

The woman was incorrigible.

Did she not understand the meaning of laying low? They were supposed to be hiding out, and it was his job to keep her out of sight. It was proving to be a difficult task.

He studied her as she continued to fold old Mr Jones' clothing. Her chin quivered, and he wondered if she was thinking about her husband. The mere act of folding the clothes of a dead man likely reminded Eleanor of her murdered husband.

If she hadn't been in hiding, she would probably be doing this same thing, but with Nathaniel's belongings. She'd at least been able to attend the funeral, under close protection, and then they'd whisked her away.

Life could be cruel.

Despite their recent days of traveling together, of their close proximity at all times, today was the first time he'd had the chance to study her. Most of his time had been taken up ensuring they weren't being followed, that no one got close enough to harm her, and she wasn't recognized.

Being such a high profile couple in Great Falls meant they were well-known. Instantly recognizable. And that didn't sit well with Glen.

At least they were far away from immediate danger now. Willowbridge was isolated and quiet. Exactly the way he liked it.

On the other hand, newcomers stood out.

"I sure could use a coffee right about now," he said, pulling his thoughts away from their grueling travel schedule. "What about you?"

She began to rise from her kneeling position and he leapt forward to help. Reaching for her hands, she slapped his away. "I can manage. I'm not useless." She scowled, and it marred her pretty face.

Eleanor was still young, around twenty-six or seven at most he guessed. Far too young to be a widow. Her long hair was pulled back with a clip, but hung loose down her back. It was obvious to anyone who cared to take the time to look, she came from money.

Her clothes, her hair, even her reticule. They were the best money could buy. He wondered how she felt about the common gowns she'd had to settle for from the store in Willowbridge. No doubt her usual attire came from the high end boutiques. Most likely in New York. Or perhaps Paris.

She glared at him for his apparent misdemeanor, which on this occasion happened to be acting like a gentleman. He might be a detective and used to fighting criminals, but he still knew how to act around a lady.

As he prepared the coffee in the kitchen, he heard her rattling through drawers in the bedroom. He had no idea why she bothered today – she would have all the time in the world to do that. There really was no rush.

The kettle finally boiled and he filled the mugs with the steaming liquid. He leaned in, breathing in the enticing aroma.

"Smells good."

She stood in the doorway, watching him. He suddenly felt awkward, like a child having been caught doing something he shouldn't. He tried to ignore the feeling, and passed one of the mugs over to her.

"It's getting late," she said, indicating the setting sun. "I should prepare something for supper."

He wondered what they might have.

She took a few sips of the hot brew, then placed her mug on the counter before rifling through the shopping. She pulled out the flour, milk, and a few other staples, then rummaged through the cupboards looking for a bowl.

He moved to what he considered a safe distance. From there he observed as she mixed all the ingredients in a large bowl with practiced precision. He still had no idea what she was making.

She turned her head and stared at him. "Pancakes," she said, as if she could read his mind. "I hope you like them."

He couldn't remember when he'd last had pancakes. He traveled a lot for his job, and mostly ate at diners and hotels. It had been a very long time since he'd had a home-cooked meal. "Of course."

She flashed him the briefest of smiles, then turned back to what she was doing.

He continued to discretely study her over the rim of his coffee mug.

"Be a sweetheart and set the table, will you?" She'd said it so casually, as though she'd said it a million times before. The suddenly distressed look on her face told him she had. To her now dead husband.

She grimaced. "Sorry," she whispered, and her pain was evident in that one little word.

"Nothing to be sorry about." He put the mug down, and did as she'd asked. He wondered how long they'd have to dance around each other.

Chapter Three

The three bedroom cottage was quaint, but cozy.

When it was time to sleep, Eleanor realized they hadn't thought this through. She'd made up the double bed where the Jones' had no doubt slept for many years, and it looked enticing.

She hadn't realized how tired she was until she'd cleaned up after supper.

The pancakes were nice, but not her best. The stress of the situation must be getting to her. Tomorrow they'd go to the Johannson Ranch and pick out a few horses. They couldn't get too many to begin with, because they had no help. Although that may change quickly as Glen had mentioned it to Sheriff Black. He promised to make enquiries on their behalf.

No doubt the quarters reserved for the cowpokes needed cleaning, so she'd deal with that tomorrow.

As she stood next to the bed, her nightgown laid out across it, she hesitated. They'd not discussed sleeping arrangements, but knew they couldn't sleep in the same bed.

In her mind, he'd always been going to sleep on the sofa. Or in one of the spare rooms. Why she hadn't mentioned it, she wasn't sure. But she was certain that's where he would sleep.

Eleanor removed the clips from her hair, and let it cascade around her shoulders.

She startled when she saw him standing in the doorway.

"You have beautiful hair," he said, giving her an appreciative glance.

She felt the color rise up her cheeks. She wasn't sure how to answer, so simply thanked him, then reached into the wardrobe. "I have some blankets and a pillow for you," she said briskly, handing them to him.

He frowned. "You surely didn't think you'd sleep here with me, did you," she asked, annoyed at his assumption they would actually live as husband and wife.

"I need to be close by to protect you. I..."

She cut him off. "The sofa or spare room is the closest you are going to get," then shoved him out of the room and slammed the door. She stood on the other side of the door, her back to it, ensuring he didn't return.

The nerve of the man! Did he honestly think she, a God-fearing, church going woman such as herself, would allow a man who was not her husband, to sleep with her?

He knocked on the door. "Eleanor," he called through the wood. "We need to talk about this."

"There's nothing to talk about," she said assertively. "Goodnight *Mr Sanders.*"

When she was certain he wouldn't try to return, she changed into her nightgown and climbed into bed.

It wasn't the most comfortable bed she'd slept in, but it was far better than sleeping upright on the trains and stagecoaches they'd had to endure for almost a week.

She closed her eyes and thought of Nathaniel. She drifted off to sleep with tears on her cheeks.

Glen stripped down to his drawers and slipped his gun under the pillow.

Not that he'd tell Eleanor, but he'd slept in worse places. Under trees, in caves, anywhere he needed to sleep.

He doubted he'd get much sleep tonight on this lumpy sofa – he needed to ensure she was safe, and he couldn't do that with his eyes closed. He might doze a little, but that was all.

When the sheriff in Great Falls had approached him to protect Mrs Eleanor Carter, they both knew it would be a difficult task. She was a woman used to getting her own way, as Glen had come to realize.

But she needed protection, and he'd drawn the short straw. He still wasn't convinced Willowbridge was the best place to keep her hidden, but that's where he was told to go, and he followed rules.

Neither of them thought they'd be here long, but it was already several weeks since her husband had died. Keeping her hidden in Great Falls had proven extremely difficult, not to mention frustrating for everyone, so the decision was made to move on.

Word on the street was they were dealing with a pair of hardened criminals who had robbed several banks, and injured people in the process. This would be their first murder.

The thought rattled him. It proved to Glen they no longer cared who they harmed. All they were interested in was the money. And if they couldn't get it from her husband, he worried they would seek her out and try to get it from Eleanor.

Of course he wouldn't tell her that. He'd convinced her the threat was low. Perhaps that wasn't a good thing, because now she wanted to traipse around town donating dead people's clothes and going to church.

His head hurt just thinking about the possibilities. About the danger she was putting herself in.

As he drifted into a light doze, her pretty face came into his mind.

Eleanor stared out the kitchen window and studied the scene before her.

It had been a long time since she had watched horses play in a paddock, and it filled her heart with joy.

She'd spent most of her childhood riding and caring for horses. She didn't want to think about the last time she'd ridden a horse – straight to the sheriff's office – and pushed the thought to the back of her mind.

"Many thanks for the coffee, Mrs Sanders."

She spun around at the unfamiliar voice behind her, and gasped. Glen sat opposite the man at the table, and studied her. Did he realize she'd forgotten about the stranger sitting in their kitchen?

Of course he did – he seemed to be able to read her mind.

Old Mr Johannson at the ranch, had mentioned Floyd Arnold as a drifter who might be willing to help out with the horses. He'd been in and around Willowbridge for over a decade, getting work where he could.

He'd arrived with the horses, and Glen had chatted with him for some time before deciding to take him on.

She stared down at her pretend husband. "You're welcome," she said. "Would you like some more cookies?"

Floyd Arnold was typical of the drifters she'd seen back home. Thin and in need of a good meal. Unlike the wanderers she'd come across before, he kept himself clean and tidy.

"We hadn't expected to get someone so soon," Glen told the man. "I don't even know the state of the worker's hut."

"We've only just arrived ourselves," Eleanor added.

Floyd looked from one to the other of them. "It was in a bad state when old Mr Jones ran the place. I don't imagine anyone has fixed it since then. Since he died, that is."

"You worked for Mr Jones? Then you know how things need to be done. Brilliant," Glen said, not even trying to hide his glee. "When we've finished our coffee, we'll wander down and take a look."

Eleanor washed and dried their few dishes, and followed the men down to the front paddock where the worker's hut stood. It took some effort to open the door, and she feared the hut would be in such a poor condition to make it uninhabitable.

She was right.

The door was almost off its hinges by the time they entered, and sunlight shone through several spaces in the roof. It needed a dust and sweep, and the bedding needed airing out.

"I thought as much," Floyd said, deflated. "But I'm used to sleeping outside. A few more days won't hurt."

"We have a spare room up in the house. You seem like a trustworthy fellow, so you can stay there until we can fix this up." The words were out of Eleanor's mouth before she could stop them.

Glen glared at her. She swallowed hard when she realized the consequences of her words.

What would this stranger think when he saw Glen sleeping on the sofa? More importantly, was he as trustworthy as they thought?

She certainly hoped so.

Glen moved to her side and pulled her close. "We're happy to have you, Floyd." He leaned down and kissed her lightly on the lips. If she hadn't been so mad with him for crossing the line, she might have enjoyed the kiss.

As she tried to pull away in protest, he held her tighter. It was as though he was punishing her for inviting this stranger into their midst.

Floyd reached up and jiggled the frames on the walls, testing their strength. Glen saw the firearm around the same time she did. Eleanor gasped.

Glen's hand hovered over his own gun, and he breached the subject. "Do you always carry a gun?"

"What? Oh, sorry. I carry it for protection. You never know who you're going to come across out here."

Glen visibly relaxed. "Especially when you're sleeping rough, I guess."

The other man grimaced. "Especially then." He went back to his inspection of the worker's hut. "I'm happy to fix this up if you've got some wood."

"There's plenty in the wood shed, and I found a bunch of tools in there too. Help yourself." His arm dropped from around her. "We'd better head back to the house." They turned to leave.

"Mr Sanders, Missus," he said, his tone serious. "I want to thank you both for the opportunity. It's been a while since I slept in a bed. It will be nice for a change."

As much as Eleanor knew she may have put them both in danger, it felt good knowing she'd done something that made a difference to someone's life.

Glen waited in the sitting room while Eleanor changed into her nightgown. Floyd had long gone to bed.

He'd spent most of the afternoon fixing up the worker's hut, but it still needed far more work. He was a good worker, Glen had to give him that.

She wasn't going to like it, but he was sleeping with her tonight. He lightly tapped on the door before entering, but didn't wait for a response.

He hoped she was decent.

"Go away," she spat as she pulled the covers up around her shoulders. "You're supposed to sleep on the sofa."

He laughed. "Since you invited Floyd to use the spare room, I can't very well do that, now can I?" he said. "We're supposed to be a married couple."

"But..." she paused, taking a deep breath. "It isn't decent," she said softly. "We're not really married."

He grinned at her sense of propriety, and Eleanor glared at him. "We have to do this, otherwise it will look suspicious," he said, then began to unbutton his shirt. She gasped then turned away from him.

He neatly folded his clothes and placed them on the nearby chair. "I'm climbing in," he said quietly, ensuring she knew what was happening in case she screamed.

The bed was comfortable. Far more comfortable than the sofa he'd slept on previously, and far more comfortable than sleeping under a tree. He pulled the covers up around himself, but would have preferred to wrap himself around the beautiful woman laying beside him.

That brought his thoughts to a halt. That sort of thinking wasn't appropriate. He'd protected many women before in his duties both as a Pinkerton Detective and a private investigator, but he'd never felt so attracted to one of his clients.

Even if she did think she was too good for him.

He knew her type – had the best of everything, mingled with high society, and filthy rich. What happened to her husband was criminal, and for her to witness it was a terrible shame. She'd never get that image out of her head, but that didn't mean she could be so self-righteous and act as though she was better than everyone else.

That kiss he planted on her earlier today – it was a spur of the moment thing. Something to let Floyd Arnold know where he stood.

Little did he know that quick kiss would leave a lasting impression on him. His fingers went to his lips at the mere thought of it.

He drifted off to sleep wondering what it would be like to share a real kiss with Eleanor Carter.

Chapter Four

Eleanor snuggled into the warm body sharing her bed. He awoke with his arm across her waist, and as she snuggled, he pulled her closer. He knew he shouldn't, but couldn't resist.

Who could? She was such a beauty.

He grinned. Did she have any idea what she was doing? She finally rolled over to face him and opened her eyes.

It was then she let out an almighty scream.

The bedroom door flew open, and a gun was aimed at the two of them. She pulled the covers up around herself and sat up. Then screamed again.

Glen reached around and put a hand across her mouth. "It's alright Eleanor. It's just Floyd." He stared down the man holding the gun. "Sorry, Floyd. My wife had a nightmare, I think. Then the gun..."

Floyd lowered his weapon.

"My apologies," he said. "When I hear a woman screaming, I can't let it be."

Glen sat up, his chest bare. "I appreciate it." His eyes scrolled down to what the man was wearing. Just his drawers. He inwardly chuckled – that would really rattle Eleanor's sensibilities.

"Mr Arnold," she said tersely, while at the same time visibly shaking. "Are you aware you are almost naked?" She averted her eyes as any well-brought up lady would. This time he chuckled out loud.

"Didn't have no time to put on anything else, Missus."

"We appreciate your help, Floyd. We really do." Glen shoved the covers back and climbed out of bed, wearing just his drawers. He wondered what Eleanor would say about that.

She slunk down under the covers, completely covering her face. He couldn't help but grin. "My wife is not used to seeing other men naked," Glen said light-heartedly.

He was rewarded with a huge smile from their would-be rescuer. "Guess I'd better cover up then," he said, laughing as he left the room.

Without dressing, Glen headed for the kitchen where he added some wood and got the fire going. He filled the kettle and placed it on the stove.

The scene before him was amazing. He'd not watched the sunrise for quite awhile, but guessed it would be his lot from now on.

At least while they lived on the ranch.

Floyd came to stand beside him. "I never fail to appreciate the sunrise," he said quietly. "It's been my drawcard to this kind of work for as long as I can remember." He was now fully dressed, which Eleanor would appreciate.

Glen turned to stare at him. "It's new to me," he said softly. "We're city folks."

The other man nodded, as though that said it all. Then he looked confused. "I thought the Missus knew horses." He scratched his head. "I figured you lived in the country."

"When she was a child," Glen answered. "She lived on a smallish horse ranch. And she's had some contact since then, so yes, *she* does." He had to make it up as he went along, but knew he was close to the mark. "I don't know horses, except to ride now and then." It wasn't untrue. He'd been shuffled from job to job by Pinkertons, but mostly traveled by train or stagecoach.

Settling in one place would be bliss, but that wouldn't be for the foreseeable future.

"Ah, water has boiled." He pulled three mugs from the cupboard and added the coffee, then took milk out of the icebox.

Eleanor wandered out, fully dressed and looking as though she hadn't just woken in terror. This woman never ceased to amaze him.

She hip bumped him to move aside, so he did.

The men both sat at the table, and she plonked a mug in front of each of them. "I assume you eat pancakes, Mr Arnold. I'm making potato pancakes with bacon on the side." It was more of a statement than a question.

His eyes lit up. "That sounds delicious, Missus. I generally just have coffee."

"Not under my roof," she said matter of factly, then headed to the pantry.

Glen studied Floyd over the top of his mug, and wondered how trustworthy this man really was. He could be a good ally if needed. He would think on that. If a gang turned up here, he may be overwhelmed. Another set of hands, another weapon in the mix – it could make all the difference.

His *wife* returned and began to mix the pancakes. "We need to organize those chickens – we're going through a lot of eggs." She snatched up three medium sized potatoes, peeled and diced them, and threw them into a pan to cook.

She looked Glen up and down and it was all he could do not to grin. "You," she said tersely. "You can go and make yourself decent. No one sits at my table without a shirt."

He couldn't help but chuckle.

She turned her back and resumed cooking. Floyd was clearly amused. "Better do what the Missus says," he whispered, then winked.

Still grinning, Glen shrugged his shoulders then deserted his coffee to go and dress.

The moment he sat back down his breakfast was placed in front of him. He leaned in to inhale the aroma. "Smells delicious, sweetheart," he said, laying it on thick for Floyd's benefit.

"It certainly does, Missus," Floyd said, agreeing.

Eleanor stared at him. "You may call me Eleanor or Mrs Car..." she stopped dead. "Uh, Mrs Sanders."

Floyd looked from one to the other of them, his expression one of utter confusion.

She looked to Glen, obviously devastated.

"We've not been married long," Glen intercepted. "My darling wife can't get used to being Mrs Sanders." He chuckled, and Floyd joined in.

Glen stood and took her in his arms. "Don't upset yourself," he said gently. "You'll get used to it."

It felt so good to hold her. Glen knew it was wrong to feel this way, but he couldn't help it. Bit by bit she was showing more of her true self than she had in weeks.

She didn't have to feed Floyd, nor did she have to provide him with a bed to sleep in. But she did both out of kindness.

With her head resting against his chest, it felt comfortable, not awkward as he'd expected. She stayed there for quite some time, and finally pulled back. She looked up into his face, and he stared at her lips.

They were there for the taking, and that's what he intended to do. To put on a show for Floyd of course. There was no other reason.

At least that's what he convinced himself.

He leaned in and gently kissed her. He knew the moment their lips connected he'd done the wrong thing. He was falling more for this woman with each passing day.

He'd been employed to do a job, and without a doubt, he was doing it. That did not include falling in love with the client.

She glared at him, then pushed herself away, reaching for her own breakfast. They said grace, then ate their meal in silence.

"What were you thinking?" She hissed under her breath when they were alone in the bedroom. Kissing her like that was unforgiveable. They were not married, and he had no right to kiss her. Or even to hold her.

That she'd enjoyed both should not come into it. The fact was, it was not proper behavior for an unmarried couple.

He took a step toward her. "It felt nice though, didn't it? Go on, admit it." She felt like slapping that smirk right off his face. "The truth is, you need to get used to it." He let his words hang between them.

"I most certainly will not." She put her hands to her hips.

He laughed again. "We are supposed to be married. Newlyweds." He got closer and snaked his arms around her waist. "And newlyweds are all over each other. Can't get enough."

She pulled her lips into a tight line, then remembered what her mother told her. It is not ladylike to do such a thing. She relaxed her mouth, then pouted.

That surely wasn't much better.

"Cute," he said, then leaned forward and kissed her again. She began to push him away, but finally relaxed into him. His arms came up her back, and he tightened his grip on her.

Her husband had been dead for less than three months and she was letting another man kiss her. Albeit a man she'd been in close proximity with for some months. He knew most of her idiosyncrasies, her likes and dislikes, and her habits, good and bad.

She shoved herself away from him. "I can't keep doing this," she said softly, her voice breaking. She turned her back to him so he wouldn't see the tears that were forming. "We are not really married. I feel as though I'm breaking my vows to Nathaniel." She sobbed, and wiped the tears from her eyes with the back of her hand.

He gently turned her to face him. "We have to do this, otherwise people will be suspicious. When people get suspicious, your cover will be broken."

"It would be different if we were really married, but we're not." Her head hurt, not from the crying, but from the thought she'd been unfaithful to her dead husband.

Glen stared at her, his expression thoughtful. "I have an idea, but I'm not sure you'll like it."

She glared at him. "If I won't like it, don't say it."

"Hear me out. We'll go into Willowbridge and get married." He put his finger to her lips as she began to protest. "When this is all over, we can get an annulment."

She pouted again and put her hands to her hips. "We're supposed to already be married. Besides, I don't want to marry you." She looked him up and down. There was certainly nothing to complain about. Mr Glen Sanders was certainly a good looking specimen. With his sky blue eyes and his blond hair, he was quite handsome.

He was tall and strong, just like a man should be.

"What say you? Shall we take a trip into town?"

Should they? She honestly didn't know what to do. Her head hurt more than ever. "Whatever will the preacher say?"

Glen pulled her close. "He will be sworn to secrecy. He has an obligation."

Eleanor had no idea if she was doing the right thing or not, but nodded in agreement.

Floyd handed Glen a list of supplies he needed to finish the repairs on the worker's hut. Once the hut was ready, Floyd could move in, and they could look at getting more horses and other trustworthy workers.

There was a lot Eleanor had planned for this place. For someone who didn't want to be here, she was becoming very comfortable with the town. Or at least with the ranch.

She put on her best dress – if she was getting married, even just for show, she was going to look the part, she'd told him. Was that a sign of her relenting or just compliance for the duration?

He may never know. What he did know, what she'd drummed into him, was it would be a marriage of convenience, and none of the benefits. One that *would* be annulled after it was all over.

He had no choice but to agree.

They headed straight to the sheriff's office, then the church. The preacher was told little, and sworn to secrecy.

The sheriff and his deputy were their witnesses, since they couldn't have anyone else witness such a covert ceremony.

Once everyone was there, the wedding ceremony was over in a matter of minutes, and the paperwork was in his hands.

Glen put his arm around his new bride, but she didn't seem happy.

He thought this would fix things, he honestly did. She was an upstanding woman, doing everything by the book, and getting married was meant to repair the rift between them.

He glanced across, and saw tears in her eyes. "This does not tarnish Nathaniel's memory," he whispered.

"I think it does," she said on a sob, and he pulled her against his chest.

"Can't cry on your wedding day," he said gently, wiping her tears with his thumb. She looked up at him with those big brown eyes and it melted his heart. "What say we celebrate at the café? Of course we won't be able to say we're celebrating."

This was his way of trying to cheer her up, but he wasn't convinced it would work.

She nodded regardless, and he watched as she straightened her shoulders and pulled herself together in a matter of moments, right in front of his eyes. Someone, most probably her mother, had really done a number on Eleanor. He'd heard women were taught all the niceties from very young, but had never seen it in action before.

He felt so bad for her. Turning her emotions off like a faucet simply wasn't natural.

Glen leaned over and shook the hands of the sheriff and deputy. "Thank you both. Your help is appreciated," he said, then invited the pair to join them at the café.

He turned to the preacher. "Thank you, Preacher, for your discretion."

The preacher didn't look as though he was convinced, but nodded in agreement. "Your secret is safe with me."

"Preacher," Sheriff Black said, then took the man aside. Glen watched as the preacher's eyes opened wide. It seemed he might now truly understand their plight.

Glen led his wife, now his real wife, out to the wagon, and helped her aboard. "We'll go to the café first, then get the rest of our supplies from the Mercantile."

He knew he was being selfish, but Glen was not unhappy about marrying his charge. Perhaps it was their many months of confinement together, or perhaps it was much more. Only time would tell.

Chapter Five

The four of them sat huddled around a table in the café – the sheriff, the deputy, Glen, and Eleanor.

They'd chosen a table in the corner, away from prying eyes and ears. Their waitress, Cherry, had taken their orders, then left them alone.

"Floyd Arnold? He's as trustworthy as they come," Sheriff David Black said quietly. They couldn't afford to have their conversations overheard. "He's lived in or around Willowbridge for most of his life. Parents owned a property about twenty miles out of town."

"When they died and the bank took over the property," Deputy Willis added, "He took to wandering. Got work wherever he could, never staying long."

Eleanor hung on every word. "He seems a nice fellow," she said, obviously feeling sorry for the man.

Glen followed the conversation carefully. He needed someone trustworthy, as well as someone he could rely on. "Suggestions for other workers when we need them?"

"No one that's available right now, but I'll send them along when I can."

Cherry interrupted to place a mug of coffee in front of each person at the table, as well as to leave a plate of cookies. "Thank you," Eleanor said softly.

There had been no new leads according to the sheriff, and as far as he could tell, no one knew Glen's wife was in Willowbridge.

His wife. It had a nice ring to it, even if it was a pretend marriage.

He'd never really wanted to marry, or thought about getting married. His lifestyle didn't make it easy. With every case, he moved to another town, and that would never work for a married man.

Being single was the best option for someone like himself. Besides, Eleanor had made it perfectly clear theirs would never be a real marriage.

When they'd finished their drinks, the three men stood. Eleanor adjusted her bonnet, and waited for Glen to pull out her chair. He was certain her former husband always did little things like that for her, and she left him in no doubt as to what she expected.

"We're off to the Mercantile now," he said as they left. He knew Eleanor had a big shopping list to fill this time, which was not a bad thing. The less she was seen in Willowbridge, the better.

Harry and Livvy Holland greeted them as though they were old friends. He could see it made Eleanor uncomfortable, but from his perspective it was good. It meant they didn't seem out of place.

Livvy followed Eleanor around with a box, filling it with the supplies she needed. "Seems like you've been cooking up a storm," Livvy commented, and Glen agreed.

"She certainly has," he said. "Potato pancakes and bacon for breakfast today. Plus we have a guest."

Livvy's eyebrows went up. "Oh? Anyone I might know?"

"Could be. We've taken on Floyd Arnold to look after things around the ranch."

"Floyd is a terrific worker, and a good man," Harry intercepted. "He'll always do right by you."

"Speaking of Floyd," Glen said. "We need timber – Floyd is repairing the worker's hut. In the meantime, he's staying in the house."

"You'll have to get the timber you want from the mill." Harry gave instructions of how to get there.

Eleanor finished her shopping and followed Livvy to the counter. "Floyd would appreciate the home cooking," Livvy said. "He's a good man, but has done it tough for quite some time."

"I thought as much," Glen said, handing over cash payment for their purchases.

Harry and Livvy glanced at each other. Perhaps he should open an account at the Mercantile. It seemed to be a point of difference, and they didn't need to make themselves standout.

"I will open an account after all," Glen said. "Here's an extra twenty dollars to start it off."

Harry took the proffered money, and again glanced at his wife. "I don't like being in debt," Glen explained, and the pair nodded.

Harry then helped carry their goods out to the wagon. "Do right by him, and Floyd will do right by you," he said quietly.

Glen thanked him and they were soon on their way to the butcher shop where they picked up enough meat to last a few days at least.

Next on the list was the timber mill, which was not far off the track on their way home. It had been a big day for both of them, and he was ready for another coffee.

Floyd helped carry the food supplies into the house, and the timber to the worker's hut. Harry was right – Floyd was a good worker.

The sheriff vouched for his honesty, and so it seemed, did Harry. That certainly put Glen's mind at ease.

"Looks like you folks been to a lot of places today," he said conversationally.

"It's been a big day, for sure. Willowbridge is bigger than I'd first realized." The pair carried the bigger pieces of timber between them, down the back to the worker's hut. "It's looking good, Floyd. You've done a great job."

"Thanks Mr Sanders. Some parts have been practically rebuilt."

"It's Glen, and I appreciate the work you've put into it. My wife and I appreciate it a lot." Floyd nodded but didn't say anything. "She's got big plans for this place. Sometimes I think they might be too big."

"Oh?"

"Horses more than anything. She wants to restore it, bring it back to what old Mr Jones had going." Glen wanted to put it out there, and find out Floyd's reaction.

"I guess that means going into competition with the Johannson Horse Ranch." Floyd scratched his head. "Not that it was ever a problem before. But being newcomers to town, he could be a might rankled."

"I hope not. But if you want it, there's plenty of work here for you. For quite a while, I'd say."

That brought a smile to Floyd's face, and for the first time, Glen noticed the real man. As Harry had mentioned, Floyd had done it tough for quite some time. Living mostly outdoors had not helped his appearance. He'd first thought the man to be in his late forties, but when he smiled, Glen could see he was more like early to mid thirties in age.

Nothing he could do about that, but perhaps he could help the man in the future. Eleanor had no plans beyond this ranch, but that could change in a heart-beat.

Neither of them knew what would happen once the outlaws were caught and she was safe again. The thought send a shiver down his spine.

Eleanor was the only woman he'd ever met who had affected him the way she did. When he touched her, a thrill went up his arm. When she was near, his heart rate accelerated. And when he kissed her, his lips tingled for the longest time.

His suggestion to marry her was not an unselfish one, far from it. But he knew he would never have a real marriage with his wife. Her heart was with Nathaniel Carter and always would be.

"Here will be fine." Floyd's voice brought him out of his thoughts, and as he turned back toward the house, Glen noticed Eleanor staring at them out of the kitchen window.

He wondered if she would ever see him as her husband and not only her protector. He tipped his hat and she immediately turned away, continuing to pack away the new supplies, most likely.

She was a good cook, which had confused him at first. He'd automatically presumed she would have had a team of servants – a cook and maid at the least.

But over time he'd come to realize she preferred to do all those tasks herself, which was probably just as well. Who else may have lost their lives that day, had they been around?

As the men returned to the house to collect more timber from the wagon, she called them in for coffee. He certainly wouldn't say no.

She placed a mug in front of each man, then added a plate of cookies to the center of the table. "They're still warm," Glen said as he reached for one. "Mmmm, yum."

Floyd grinned and took a bite of his cookie. "These are delicious, Missus. Uh, Missus Sanders," he amended. "Thank you. It's a long time since I've had homemade cookies."

"She's a good cook, my wife," added Glen. He couldn't wipe the grin off his face if he wanted to.

"My mother taught me to cook," she said quietly. "Growing up on a horse ranch meant we girls had to help with the cooking and household chores." She looked thoughtful. "Then there were the horses..."

For the first time, Glen saw how vulnerable Eleanor really was. Not defenseless like when Floyd came running in with his weapon drawn, but like a woman remembering special times from her childhood. Times she believed she'd never have again.

This was not the strong woman he'd protected over the past months. Perhaps her true self was finally showing itself.

Floyd stared at her momentarily, taking it all in, then ate the rest of his cookie and gulped down his coffee. "Back to work," he said, snatching up another oatmeal cookie as he went. He certainly seemed more content these last few days.

Glen couldn't imagine living the life of an itinerant worker. Not knowing where your next meal was coming from or if you'd have somewhere decent to sleep.

Harry and the sheriff were both right. He was a good man and a hard worker, and Glen intended to reward him for that with the promise of a job for as long as there was one available.

The men finished moving the timber to the back of the property – it was obvious Floyd would be staying with them in the ranch house for some time to come. That was not necessarily a bad thing.

"Darn it," Glen said out of the blue. "I forgot to ask about chickens."

"Chickens?" Floyd scratched his head.

"For the chicken coop. Eleanor has her heart set on raising chickens."

Floyd grinned. "I know a few places I can get you some."

"Legally?" Glen wasn't certain everything Floyd did was above board.

The other man chuckled. "I can do that too. We can get them this afternoon if you like."

Glen couldn't risk leaving Eleanor alone. Wouldn't risk it. "I can't leave my wife alone – she is frightened of being by herself. But don't tell her I said so."

"She scares easily, the Missus," Floyd said.

"Unfortunately, yes. But she's improving." He pulled some notes out of his wallet. "Will that cover it?"

"Should be more than enough."

Floyd headed for the wagon, and Glen for the house. The aroma of supper cooking hit him as he entered the kitchen. "Stew? Smells good."

Eleanor threw the last of the vegetables in the pot with the meat and stirred them. "It does, doesn't it?" She smiled and his heart did a little flutter. "I thought biscuits would go nicely with the stew." She indicated to a tray on the counter with biscuits waiting to go in the oven.

"You're spoiling us," Glen said, pulling her close.

She pushed him away. "Where's Floyd gone?"

"It's a surprise," he told her. "Eleanor," he said softly, totally changing the subject. "I really like holding you."

She grimaced. "I like it too, but we agreed to a marriage of convenience."

He pulled her close again. "If we're to pull this off, we must act like a real married couple." He glanced down at her face. All of the softness was gone, and he was sure she would baulk again, but she didn't.

Instead she leaned into him. "I miss Nathaniel," she said quietly.

When Glen glanced down, a tear trickled down her face.

He wiped it away with his thumb. "I know you do. And I'm not trying to replace him, I promise. My intention has always been to keep you safe."

She snuggled into him again. It felt nice, and he could certainly take more of this. Unfortunately, she was mostly an unwilling participant.

Chapter Six

Eleanor snuggled into Glen and it felt good.

She couldn't believe she'd done that. It felt comforting when she snuggled like that, so she stayed right where she was.

He was right, they had to appear to be a happily married couple. They were married, but happily was far from the truth.

Last night was the first time she'd slept well since Nathaniel's murder. Having Glen in the bed with her gave her a sense of security. Perhaps it was a false sense of security, but she'd slept better, nonetheless.

She heard him swallow and looked up. He gazed into her eyes and pulled her a little closer, held her a little tighter.

She felt safe with Glen, and had done so from the very beginning. When the sheriff suggested they put her into protective custody she'd baulked, but finally agreed. His cousin Glen had done it before, the sheriff said.

It turned out he was an ex-Pinkertons detective, and only took on occasional work. Luckily for her he took her on, because she had no idea where she would be now, or how safe she would be.

The investigation was ongoing, but she wished they would find the killers and let her get back to her normal life. A life that no longer included Nathaniel.

Glen stared into her face. "Are you alright?"

She nodded. "I, I was thinking about Nathaniel," she said quietly, then pulled out of his arms to stir the stew. "What's all this about a surprise?" She turned back to face him.

"I've sent Floyd to collect it. It should be here soon."

She went to the window and stared out. "It's so nice to see horses running around the paddock. I've really missed that." She spun around to face him. "Do you ride?"

He stared at her then laughed. "Not if I can help it."

She grimaced. "I adore riding. I want to go riding soon." She put her hand up before he could protest. "I'm going with or without you."

Eleanor knew she'd given him no choice. "I can teach you."

He frowned and stared her down. "I have ridden before, you know. I just prefer not to."

She knew there were people like him around – people who didn't particularly like horses. She had never understood it, and probably never would. Having been brought up on a horse farm concreted her future in that regard.

She snatched up some apples and shoved them into the pocket of her skirts, then headed for the back door.

"Where are you going?" he asked as she opened the door.

She swiveled her head and glanced at him over her shoulder. "I'm going to visit the horses. You're welcome to tag along."

He screwed up his nose and she laughed.

It felt good. She hadn't laughed much over the past few months. In fact, she couldn't recall even one time she'd laughed since she'd lost Nathaniel.

That thought sobered her almost immediately. She preferred the feeling of happiness, and continued toward the back paddock where the horses ran free.

She heard Glen behind her and when he finally caught up, covered her hand with his. A thrill went through her, until she remembered what he'd said about behaving like a happily married couple.

It was all for show. He had no feelings whatsoever toward her, and it was mutual. Sure, she liked snuggling into him, but it meant nothing.

Nothing more than being a source of comfort that was. But he held her like she meant something to him, but she was certain that wasn't true.

It was all part of the job. It's what she paid him for anyway. To put on a good show so no one would suspect they weren't really married.

That brought her up quick. *They were really married.* As of this morning she was Mrs Glen Sanders.

She was no longer Eleanor Carter, wife of the slain banker, Nathaniel Carter.

Her breath caught in her throat. *What had she done?*

They finally reached the fence to the paddock, and one of the horses galloped over to her. He nudged his nose into her shoulder and whinnied. Then he moved his head toward her pocket and sniffed.

"Hello boy," she said gently, at the same time laughing, then reached into her pocket. He greedily ate the apple she offered, and whinnied into her shoulder again when he was finished.

"He likes you." Glen's voice pulled her away from the beautiful boy standing in front of her.

She smiled at him. "I like him too." She thought for a moment. "I need to find a name for him." She closed her eyes trying to come up with an appropriate name. "I know, Fury." She reached up and rubbed her hand up and down his nose.

"He likes that."

"Yes he does." She turned to Glen. "Fury will be mine. He's not to be sold when we get to that stage."

The other horses realized she had treats and made their way to the fence. A few nuzzled into her shoulder, and she reached into her pocket again. Fury didn't budge, and fought his way closer to get another bite or two.

"I think he'll live up to his name." Fury suddenly reared up and whinnied. Eleanor turned to see what the fuss was about, and saw Floyd enter the yard carrying a crate. "What's that?" she asked. "Oooh, is it my surprise?"

"It most certainly is, my love."

She flinched at his easy use of the words, but said nothing. They made their way back to the house and Floyd.

Her heart raced when she saw what was inside the crate. Chickens! Her surprise was chickens! "Oh Glen, that's so wonderful." She turned and wrapped her arms around him. "Thank you," she whispered in his ear.

"Excuse me, Missus Sanders." She glanced across to Floyd, who was beaming at her, obviously happy with his part in this conspiracy. "Should I let them loose or lock them up?"

"Let them run loose. Oooh, this is so exciting!" She turned to Glen and hugged him again. "I've really missed having chickens, and fresh eggs."

Glen squeezed her, as though he understood her excitement. "I must go and check on the supper."

She reluctantly left the men to let the chickens loose. It turned out to be an amazing day, even if it had begun with her marrying a man she didn't love and barely knew.

The stew was mouth-watering, along with the biscuits.

"This is good, really good, Missus," Floyd said when he'd emptied his mouth. "I haven't had such good food for quite a while."

Eleanor blushed at the compliment. It was cute. The pink in her cheeks suited her, and the fact she blushed at praise reinforced Glen's belief that her haughty behavior was all for show.

"It most certainly is," Glen echoed. "You are a wonderful cook, sweetheart."

She blushed again, this time trying to hide it by putting her hands to her cheeks. "I, I made apple and rhubarb pie for dessert," she said, obviously trying to divert attention away from herself.

"My goodness," Floyd blurted out. "I cannot believe my luck, landing a job here."

Glen glanced across at him. "We're the lucky ones, Floyd. Finding someone as hard working and conscientious as yourself."

Now it was Floyd's turn to blush. Trying to cover up, he lifted his coffee mug. If he didn't know better, Glen would have thought there were tears in the other man's eyes.

"You're already like part of the family," Eleanor told him, and Glen could see she genuinely meant it.

"Speaking of family, when I was out getting the chickens today, I heard there's a dance coming up in Willowbridge."

Glen glanced across at Eleanor. There was panic in her eyes. "Sounds good, but I'm not sure if we'll go."

"That's a shame," the other man said. "They're only on every couple of months. You'd get to meet the other residents of Willowbridge."

Eleanor shook her head. She was determined not to go.

"It's a church event." Floyd continued to tuck into his stew and biscuits.

Eleanor's head shot up. "We probably should go then," she said, and Glen knew how hard that must have been for her. "I, I'm not good with people though, so probably won't."

As was his norm, Floyd didn't judge. "That's a shame," he said, and took another mouthful of food.

Glen was thoughtful. Should they risk going out in public to learn who was living in Willowbridge? If the killers were here somewhere, this event might bring them out.

On the other hand, he didn't want to risk Eleanor's life. This could be a way to draw the killer's out, and let her finally get on with her life.

It could also mean an annulment of their marriage and the parting of ways. He wasn't sure he was willing to take that risk.

With the sheriff on side, the decision was made to attend the dance.

Deputy Willis would also be there, so that made three of them looking out for Eleanor. Floyd would also help if needed, he was certain.

Eleanor was still far from convinced it was a good idea. She was more concerned about the welfare of the rest of the town folks than for her own life. None of which surprised Glen.

For someone who came from money, she was a most unselfish woman.

She'd been baking for most of the day, and Glen had breathed in the aromas. "It's a long time since I've enjoyed a job so much," he'd whispered as he came up behind her.

She startled, and he wrapped his arms around her. Despite the fact they'd married, except for snuggling into him when Floyd was around, she didn't act like they were married.

She kept her distance in the bed, preferring to move to the far side. Sometimes he wondered if she would fall out. Despite that, they awoke each morning wrapped in each other's arms.

He wasn't complaining.

Waking up to her every day was something he could certainly get used to. In fact, he had already gotten used to it, and didn't want it to end.

He'd spent most of his adult life chasing criminals and protecting damsels in distress. The latter had been his lot for the last few years since he'd decided to quit his job at Pinkertons. As much as he'd enjoyed his job, he didn't like the constant travel. He also didn't like being shot at on a regular basis.

Living out here on a ranch in Willowbridge, suited him perfectly. He could happily live out the rest of his days here, on one proviso. That Eleanor was by his side.

She was beautiful, caring, and if she'd let herself, he knew she could be very loving.

He didn't care about her money. Glen had plenty of his own. His work had always included all expenses paid, so he'd squirreled away the rest. He had enough money to buy this ranch one hundred times over.

"Mmmmm."

He looked down into her face as she groaned in her sleep. Her lips looked so delicious, so enticing. He slowly moved toward them, ready to kiss her.

Her eyes fluttered open.

"What are you doing?" she asked, obviously startled.

He stayed exactly where he was, still hovering over her mouth. "I was about to kiss you," he said, his voice husky.

"Well don't." She slid sideways and out of the bed. "That wasn't part of our agreement."

Her words stung, but he knew it was true. He glanced across to her, and was surprised to see the disappointment on her face.

Was she beginning to have feelings for him? Glen shook that thought away. Surely it wasn't true? She was adamant he not touch her when Floyd wasn't around, but it hadn't deterred him so far.

He quickly jumped out of bed, and she stared at his bare chest. He stood in front of her wearing only his drawers. She stared, but didn't say a word.

Instead she pulled her robe around herself. Despite his agreement, he longed to hold her like any man would want to hold his wife.

But Eleanor was having none of it when they were alone. He desperately wanted to break down her defenses.

He fully understood her reckoning. She'd already lost one husband, and so wanted to keep her distance. When he'd suggested they marry, he hadn't done it purely to keep her safe. He'd hoped it would eventually break down the barriers between them.

So far that hadn't worked. Well, maybe a little, but not enough for his liking.

"Don't just stand there," she said abruptly. "We have work to do. A ranch doesn't run itself, you know."

She suddenly looked shocked.

"What are you thinking," he asked gently.

Her chin quivered. "About my mother. That's what she used to say."

He stepped toward her and she wrapped her arms around him, leaning her head on his bare chest. Warm tears fell against his skin.

His hands went up her back and he rubbed them in circles, attempting to comfort her.

"This isn't only about your mother, is it?" he asked gently. "It's about everything that's happened in the past few months."

She glanced up at him, her chin still quivering. "I'm scared," she said. It was the first time she'd admitted her true feelings to him.

She was at her most vulnerable right now. He felt bad, because that was on him. "I know you are," he said, touching her lips with his fingers. "I promise, we will keep you safe."

He continued to rub his hands over her back, until she looked up at him with those pleading brown eyes and asked him to kiss her.

And so he did.

Chapter Seven

Eleanor had only been fooling herself.

All this time she'd denied her feelings for Glen. For her husband.

There was one reason, and one reason only – she didn't want to tarnish Nathaniel's memory. They'd had a good life together, but their marriage had been short. Little more than a year.

When she thought about it, Eleanor realized she hadn't really known him.

She stood staring out the kitchen window, enjoying watching the horses prance across the paddock. She'd still not enticed Glen onto a horse, but she was working on it. She loved to ride – it was freeing to her, and she missed it.

Back in Great Falls she rode almost daily. Sometimes bareback – her most favorite way to ride. Nathaniel insisted she didn't ride when he wasn't there, in case she fell he always said, but refused to ride with her. If she wasn't back by a certain time, he would come looking for her.

When she wanted to go shopping, he accompanied her. And he demanded she stay at home when he was at work. She also had to keep the doors locked - for her safety, he said.

He was always looking out for her.

Or was he? She was beginning to think their marriage may not have been all she thought it was. Glen didn't place restrictions on her, except to stay close, but that was for her protection.

She was collecting eggs for the day's baking when she heard horses out the front. They never had visitors.

Glen and Floyd were at the worker's hut doing repairs.

Glen had forbidden her to open the door, even if she thought she knew who was there. She called out to him and he came running.

Floyd gave her a strange look, and her thoughts went to what he must think of her unusual behavior.

"I heard horses out the front," she told Glen in a panic when he got closer.

He held her by the shoulders to reassure her, and kissed her gently on the cheek.

They went inside the house, leaving Floyd out the back to continue his work. Glen moved the curtains slightly to check who was there. It was the sheriff and deputy.

They breathed a collective sigh of relief, then let them in.

Sheriff Black looked excited. Then he glanced at Eleanor and his excitement seemed to evaporate. "I have news," he said, then glanced at Eleanor again.

They waited expectantly but nothing more came.

"Whatever you have to say, Sheriff, you can say in front of me." She was in a huff, that much was evident.

She waved them over to the sitting room chairs, and offered them coffee, then left the room. Still annoyed the sheriff didn't want to share his news with her.

She could hear voices coming from the other room, but couldn't make out the words. What were they saying? What was the news the sheriff was so excited about?

Eleanor returned with a tray of coffee-filled mugs and a plate of cookies.

All eyes turned to her, and dread filled her.

She handed out the drinks, fulfilling her obligation as hostess before sitting down and asking the obvious question. "So what is the news," she asked, her voice even, ensuring her emotions didn't trip her up.

Both their guests turned to Glen, silently begging him to be the bearer of the bad news. It was bad news, she was certain. Otherwise, why were they so reluctant to tell her?

"For goodness sakes," she said, quite annoyed at the silence in the room. "Somebody tell me."

She looked from one to the other. Why were they so reluctant to speak to her? "Glen?"

He rubbed his hand across his stubbled chin. "It's about Nathaniel." He stared at her as though he was sizing her up. "It appears he may have been complicit in a planned robbery at his bank. The sheriff in Great Falls believes he backed out at the last minute, which is why he was murdered."

Her heart thumped in her chest. *Surely that wasn't true? Nathaniel wouldn't do such a thing. Would he?*

She quietly placed her mug on a side table with shaky hands, then stood. "Excuse me," she said, voice shaking and her head spinning. Eleanor walked toward the kitchen to go outside and get some air. The last thing she remembered was Glen catching her as she fainted.

No matter how many times he tried to discuss what had happened, Eleanor found a way around it. She didn't want to know her former husband may have been involved in a planned bank robbery.

Glen wasn't a cruel man, but he needed his wife to understand the implications. Nathaniel had apparently backed out, and was killed for his troubles.

Eleanor was extremely lucky to be alive. At least that's what he believed.

Since the revelations about her former husband, she hadn't mentioned him. Not even once. Glen already had a lot of empathy for her, but now it was ten-fold. He couldn't begin to imagine how dreadful she must feel.

She'd kept herself busy baking, cleaning the house, and doing laundry. She also spent a lot of time watching the horses from the fence of the paddock.

She almost constantly annoyed Glen to go riding, but he'd resisted. It wasn't his favorite past-time. Besides he wasn't sure how safe she would be.

Glen came up behind her and wrapped his arms around her. "Want to go riding?" He wanted to draw her out of her misery, and as much as he hated riding, he wanted to see her happy.

She spun around in his arms. "Can we? That would be marvelous!" She seemed more excited than she'd been in a very long time.

She hugged him, and he reveled in her nearness. In the days since the sheriff had visited, she'd kept her distance. He knew it wasn't him – it was Eleanor dwelling on the past.

He hoped this would be a turning point. She looked up at him with those big brown eyes. "About Nathanial," she said, her eyes glistening.

Glen leaned into her and kissed her cheek. "We don't have to talk about him if you don't want to." She nodded then held him tight.

"Then let's not." She stayed there for a few minutes, which he reveled in, then pushed out of his arms and headed for the house. He knew well what she'd be doing – cutting up apples and carrots for the horses. Fury in particular had become very used to being spoiled.

Glen sent Floyd to collect Fury and another horse for Glen. He didn't like Eleanor going into the paddock. They had no idea how the horses would react, but Floyd had dealt with them before, so knew them reasonably well.

He entered the paddock with two sets of reins, and soon had them ready to be dressed. Glen helped him once they were back in the stables.

"This horse, Fury," Glen said, matter of factly. "Can he be trusted?"

Floyd glanced at him. "One of the best. Hasn't been ridden a lot from what I remember, but if anyone can handle him, it's the Missus."

"What about this one?" He indicated the second horse Floyd had led into the stables.

"The Missus calls this one Winston - he's pretty calm. Probably what you need since you're not so experienced." Glen glared at him, then felt guilty.

What Floyd said was true. He only rode when he absolutely had to.

Eleanor joined them, and Floyd helped her up onto the saddle. Glen managed by himself.

"Don't get lost," Floyd told them. "Are you certain you'll be alright? You don't know these parts."

Glen glanced across at his wife. She chewed on her bottom lip. She only did that when she was anxious.

"On second thoughts, perhaps you should come along."

Floyd rounded up another horse, this one called Temper, and saddled it. Then they set off across their property.

Glen glanced across at Eleanor. She was in her element.

She sat tall on Fury, her hands relaxed in the reins. She'd yanked her skirts up around her legs like she'd done it a thousand times before, and she probably had. She didn't seem to care that Floyd could see her bare legs, let alone her ankles.

Glen was enjoying it, but would prefer the other man didn't.

They started out at a slow walk, but Eleanor was quickly impatient and moved into a trot. The ranch property was large, much larger than Glen had originally anticipated. As they got further away from the house, Eleanor reached up and pulled the clip out of her hair, letting it flow freely across her back and shoulders.

Something inside Glen shimmied, and he couldn't help but stare. This beautiful woman was his wife.

He tried to forget it was just for show.

He watched mesmerized as the wind blew her hair in the air and across her face. She shook her head to let it run free. He wished he was close enough to run his hands through it – then he remembered Floyd.

The ranch hand hung back at a big enough distance to give them privacy, and Glen moved closer to Eleanor and Fury. As he got closer, she began to canter, and Glen urged his horse to do the same. Pretty soon she was galloping, and was too far ahead for his liking.

"Eleanor," he called loudly. "Slow down." But she totally ignored him.

They soon came to a stand of trees and she slowed, then entered the forest-like area. "Seriously Eleanor, you need to stop."

He was getting frustrated with her now, because she would soon be out of sight, and he would not be in control if something happened. Floyd came up beside him, and they continued on together.

"I don't think the Missus realizes there could be rattlers in there," he said, looking decidedly worried.

"Damn it," Glen said, urging his horse forward.

When they found her a few minutes later, Eleanor was no longer in the saddle. She was standing in front of Fury, one hand to the horse's face and the other feeding him pieces of carrot.

It was a sight to behold, and Glen's heart did a little skip. The love between rider and horse was evident. He dearly wanted to enjoy that same sort of relationship with his wife.

They arrived at the dance early, before practically anyone else.

Glen wanted to see the layout of the place in case some catastrophe occurred and he needed to know his way around.

Floyd came with them on the wagon – they couldn't deny him this night. He was one of the family now.

Eleanor packed up all her baked goods, their contribution to the night. He was certain she'd gone overboard, but she was having none of it.

Apple pie, raspberry jam slice, and a batch of blueberry muffins. She'd made two lots of each – one each for the dance, and another to leave at home. He wasn't complaining.

He'd come to realize baking was Eleanor's way of reducing stress. If that's what made her feel more calm, then he was all for it.

She'd put on her Sunday best gown, which she usually reserved for church. She'd insisted she needed to look her best for the dance.

If that's what made her happy, then so be it.

When this was all over, no doubt she'd order more gowns from her favorite boutique. Right now though, it was simply too dangerous.

He'd watched as she brushed her long flowing hair and tied it back. No matter what she did with it, she always looked beautiful. And refined. His Eleanor was an elegant lady and that could never be disputed.

When they were ready to leave, he handed her a shawl. She looked at him questioningly. "It might be warm now, but it can be quite brisk in Willowbridge at night," he said.

She nodded. She'd said barely a word all day, and he knew it was because she was scared. More fearful than she'd been the entire time he'd been protecting her.

As they entered the building, the sheriff and deputy came toward them. "All checked out and clear," Sheriff Black told him.

"Thanks, but if you don't mind, I'd like to double-check." He knew they wouldn't be offended. They'd do the same themselves in his position.

Eleanor sat on the sidelines talking to Floyd. "Keep an eye out while I do my checks?" The men nodded. There were few people in Willowbridge he trusted right now, mostly because he didn't know them, but these two he would bet his life on. Heck, he'd just bet Eleanor's life on them.

The musicians were beginning to warm up, and parishioners were arriving. Not many at this point, but they would soon, he was certain. That's when he would need to be vigilant.

The more crowded it became, the more stressed Eleanor was.

Floyd continued to sit and talk with her, and outwardly all seemed as it should be, but he knew her well. She didn't have to tell him, it was written all over her face. The softness had disappeared, and worry lines appeared around her eyes. Her fists were clenched too.

He sat next to her, his eyes on the crowd. Any wrong move and he'd be on it. He felt suddenly compelled to stand. "Would you like to dance?" He reached out and took Eleanor's hands in his own. She seemed reluctant at first, but then agreed.

They moved onto the dance floor, and she leaned into him. This time she didn't flinch. "How are you holding up," he asked quietly.

She looked up at him, those beautiful brown eyes mesmerizing him. "I'm fine. Floyd keeping me company is helping."

He pulled her closer and felt her relax against him. He could do this all night. Every day they were together, he felt himself falling more and more in love with his wife.

Chapter Eight

Eleanor reveled in their nearness.

She'd kept Glen at a distance in reverence to Nathanial. But now she'd found out what sort of person he really was, she no longer felt any sense of loyalty toward him.

Glen was a wonderful man, and she enjoyed having him around. Not only because he protected and looked out for her. He had so many good attributes, and she couldn't think of a single bad one.

Unless you counted walking around bare chested. He seemed to like doing that. Sometimes she wondered if he only did it to taunt her.

She smiled at the thought.

She wrapped her arms tighter around him and swayed to the gentle music. She'd missed going to balls and dances and other social events. But the circumstances of the past months had turned her into a recluse of sorts.

She didn't know people here, and felt rather out of place.

Eleanor rested her head against Glen's chest and enjoyed the moment. Why had she been so reluctant to come tonight?

The first reason was obvious – she could very well be killed by Nathanial's killers. The second was because she knew so few people.

She was happy and comfortable right where she was. "You look content." She startled when Glen whispered in her ear, then nodded.

"I am." She looked up at him. "I am very comfortable, and could stay here forever." She gazed into his eyes. They were as blue as sapphires.

She reached up and put her hand to his cheek, gently stroking it. He caught her hand with his own. A thrill went through her, and she was confused.

All this time she'd pushed him away, not wanting to get close to him. Now she knew the truth about her former husband, and Eleanor could only assume she'd let her guard down. Now, more than ever, she wanted Glen to touch her.

They stared into each other's eyes, and she wondered if he was thinking the same thing. "Music stopped," he whispered. "We should sit down again."

Before they had the chance, Livvy and Harry Holland from the Mercantile approached them. They chatted about nothing for awhile, then introduced them to a few of the other town folk. Some they'd met briefly in the various stores, others were new to them.

One thing Eleanor did know, and that was she'd never remember all their names. Not yet anyway.

The music began again, and Glen used it as an excuse for them to get away. She was feeling decidedly uncomfortable with all these people approaching her, and he'd obviously picked up on it.

She figured Glen had learned to read her a long time ago, but thought it was probably part of his job.

Eleanor didn't want to mingle, she just wanted to dance with her husband. She pushed closer to him, and could feel the taut muscles of his stomach. Her hands ran up his arms, and as she held them, she felt the strong muscles there too.

It almost took her breath away.

Soon the music stopped and an announcement was made the food was ready to eat. She smiled as she watched Floyd clamber toward the food tables. Floyd certainly liked his food.

She studied him as he collected up food, and chatted to some of the other town folk, then froze in horror as he indicated her way. Glen reached for her hand, and squeezed it, then slipped his arm around her back.

"Just breathe," he said. "That's the mill owner, remember?" She hadn't remembered. She'd barely noticed him when they were there. Eleanor was tired and had been anxious to leave.

It had been a long night for her, and once the men had eaten enough, she almost begged to leave. Eleanor felt extremely uncomfortable, felt as though there were eyes on her. It almost burned a hole in her back. But she didn't tell Glen until finally she felt compelled to.

"Glen," she said, standing. "We must leave." He studied her face, then cupped her cheeks with his hands.

He suddenly looked worried. "Tell me what's got you so scared all of a sudden."

When she told him, he reacted immediately. "Floyd, can you get the sheriff and deputy for me, please?"

Now Floyd looked worried. "Is everything alright, Missus?" She said nothing, but leaned into her husband.

Eleanor knew she could rely on them, but now felt terrified of what might happen. She was not only scared for herself, but for Glen and everyone else in the room. "We have to leave," she said urgently.

Glen glanced around the room. "Do you see them here?" She followed his lead but couldn't see the men who killed her former husband. She shook her head.

The sheriff and deputy approached, and the men formed a huddle around her, discussing their course of action.

She couldn't breathe. Between her panic and no air from being caught in the huddle, she felt light-headed. Eleanor pushed her way out. Then she screamed.

Standing just feet away was one of the killers, and he had a gun aimed at her. "Hello Mrs Carter," he said with a sneer on his face. Before she knew what was happening, Glen was in front of her, shoving her out of the way. Floyd caught her before she could fall, and looked totally confused.

A gun went off, and she screamed again. Other women also screamed around them, and people scattered in all directions.

Glen was on the ground. Eleanor knew if he hadn't taken a bullet for her, she would be dead now, shot in the head. The thought she could be dead now was painful, but not as painful as the thought of losing the man she'd come to love.

Suddenly there was a scuffle, and Eleanor watched on in horror. It wasn't long before the sheriff and deputy had the man restrained.

She watched on as Glen spotted a second man. He was running in the opposite direction, a gun hanging by his side. Despite the bullet to the shoulder, despite the agony he must have been in,

Glen reached for his gun and hit his target at the first attempt.

Tears rolled down Eleanor's cheeks as she ripped part of her skirts to put pressure on his bullet ridden shoulder. She leaned over her husband and looked down into his pain-filled face. "Don't die, Glen," she sobbed. "Please don't die. I love you so much - I couldn't bare to lose you."

He stared into her eyes, they were filled with unshed tears. "I love you too," he said quietly, moments before his eyes fluttered closed and Doc Matlock arrived to take care of him.

"You shouldn't have done it," Eleanor argued.

Floyd also sat at the table, but was grinning. "It's not funny," she said, directing her words to Floyd this time.

"He would have killed you," Glen said. "I've taken bullets before, and I'm still here."

She glared at him. "This time could have been your last. You're just lucky he didn't hit vital organs." Her eyes filled with tears. "I don't know what I would do without you." She suddenly went quiet and her chin quivered.

Floyd grabbed his mug of coffee and went outside, leaving them alone.

Despite now knowing the full story, knowing the danger they'd put him in, Floyd still wanted to stay with them on the ranch. Glen couldn't tell him how long that would be, since it was dependent on Eleanor's decision about their future.

If it was his choice, they'd never leave.

Glen stood and wrapped his arms around his wife. She leaned against him, and Glen reveled in her nearness.

The rest of his life depended on her decision. Would she stay or would she go? Would they stay married or did she want an annulment?

Glen hoped and prayed they would be together for the rest of their lives.

Epilogue

Eleanor patted her slightly protruding belly and looked around at the good people of Willowbridge.

They'd congregated at the ranch to witness the renaming. It no longer seemed appropriate for everyone to call it the old Jones ranch.

Instead it had become known as the Glenellie property.

As they did in Willowbridge, the day was made into a special celebration with each family bringing food to share. Eleanor stifled a laugh as she watched Floyd run his eyes over the food tables he and Glen had set out for that purpose.

Glen had commissioned a wooden plaque from Alex Mason, the local carpenter, and it was more beautiful than she had expected. The ranch name was burned into the wood with decorative flourishes around it.

There were tears in her eyes when Alex showed it to them. Glen had pulled her close, as he loved to do every chance he got.

With no more threat to her life, Eleanor had come to love the quaint little town of Willowbridge, and all the people in it.

She looked out across the sea of faces. Harry and Livvy Holland were there, Alex and his wife Harriet, and Cherry from the Café, as well as her children. The sheriff and Deputy Willis, Pops from the Livery, and also Jackson Hillside who ran the stagecoach. To name just a few.

Eleanor had joined the ladies auxiliary, and was enjoying the social aspect of the group. They helped out those who needed it, and that's what mattered most to her.

"If I can get the attention of you good folks," Floyd said, speaking more loudly than Eleanor had ever heard. Everyone stopped talking and looked his way. "We are all here today to officially welcome the Missus and Glen to Willowbridge."

It was all she could do to stifle a grin. After all this time, Floyd still called her Missus. It was a term of endearment, so she really didn't mind. Floyd was now well entrenched in their little family, which had recently grown. Once the worker's hut was fully repaired, they'd hired more cowboys and made Floyd foreman. He more than deserved it.

He turned toward the posts he'd erected and placed the plaque on. It was currently covered, but would soon be unveiled.

Eleanor's thoughts went back to the day they'd arrived, and how disgusted she was at her new home. With a bit of hard work and determination, Glen and Floyd had turned it into a place she loved.

They'd been working on the nursery too, including a crib for the baby. And not a moment too soon. It wouldn't be long and their family would expand.

"I'm also going to take this here opportunity to thank the Missus and Glen for making me feel like part of their family," he added.

He pulled the covering off the plaque to a round of applause. "Right then, I reckon it's time to eat," he said.

Eleanor couldn't help but grin. That was true to form for Floyd. Eating was his most favorite thing to do.

Everyone gathered around the tables, and Glen guided her to a chair. She wasn't far into her confinement and he was already being far more fussy than was necessary.

Livvy Holland came up to her. "You're glowing, Eleanor. You look even more beautiful than usual." That made her blush.

She realized how very lucky she was to live in this wonderful town called Willowbridge. And how blessed she was to have a husband like Glen.

Eleanor was tired. She'd fussed around for days wanting to finish the nursery before the baby arrived, but they still had a few weeks.

Glen told her so, but she still fussed.

She was sitting in a rocking chair in the nursery when he got back from the post office. "There's a letter for you," he said. "Return address says it's from your sister, Cassandra."

That would fill her heart with joy for sure. Cassandra had said she'd come and help once the baby was born. Eleanor ripped the envelope open and began to read.

She'd slowed down a lot lately, and when he'd checked, Doc Matlock said it was normal this late in the confinement. Right now she seemed happy enough. Getting mail from her sister had certainly cheered her up.

Her eyes scanned the writing. "Cassandra says she will be here before Christmas," she said cheerfully. She glanced at Glen. "That will be lovely. I haven't seen Cassandra since well before Nathanial was murdered."

She closed her eyes briefly, and he knew she was reliving that day. "Let's get you into bed for a good rest." He reached out and took both her hands.

"Can I at least have a cup of tea first?"

"I'll bring it to you in bed." She looked exhausted and Glen didn't want to take any chances.

Eleanor shook her head. "I'm not an invalid, Glen. I'm with child." Her eyes appealed to him and he felt sorry for her. Being so active normally, this confinement must be frustrating for her.

"Alright, but only to drink tea, and then to bed."

She audibly sighed. "You go and do whatever you need to do. I'll be fine."

He respectfully declined.

Floyd and the boys were more than capable of looking after the horses. The chickens mostly took care of themselves, and their little vegetable patch needed little to no interference at all.

The kettle was already on the verge of boiling, so he pulled the mugs down out of the cupboard. Eleanor sat comfortably in the sitting room while she waited – Glen had won, and was making tea for her.

"I found some cookies in the cupboard," he said, placing the cookie-filled plate on the table next to her.

When he glanced across, she grimaced. "Something's not right," she whispered, her eyes on the brink of tears. "It's too early – the baby can't come yet." Tears rolled down her cheeks, Eleanor no longer able to hold back her emotions.

She held out both hands and he helped her to her feet. "Let's get you to bed and I'll get Doc Matlock out here."

As she stood her waters broke. "No, no, no! This can't happen now – it's too early!" Her words came out between sobs, and Glen pulled her to him, running his fingers through her hair.

His heart was pounding. She was right – it was far too early. He reached down and lifted her, then carried her to the bed. "Stay here. I won't be long."

He ran outside in near panic, calling for Floyd to go to Willowbridge and hurry back with the doctor. He'd never seen Floyd move so quickly.

By the time he returned inside, Eleanor was screaming in pain. "The baby is coming," she said between screams. "It's too early!"

Glen sat on the side of the bed trying to calm his wife. He felt totally helpless and was at a loss of what to do.

She grabbed at his hands and held them tight. "Arrrrrrrrrrrrrrrrrgh!"

Her screaming near broke his heart. "The baby can't come yet," she said between screams.

He agreed but couldn't tell her so. "It will be alright," he said, running his fingers through her hair. "Try to keep calm."

She glared at him.

It felt like hours before the doc arrived, but he knew it to be much less time.

"Thanks for coming, Doc," Glen said as Doc Matlock rushed through the door. He explained what had happened so far, and was promptly told to leave. He felt deflated.

"No, wait," the Doc said as he placed his hand on the door handle. "Get some clean towels, and a bowl of boiling water."

"Sure thing, Doc." Glen rushed out of the room and returned a short time later – just in time to hear Eleanor scream one last time.

"Hand me a towel, Glen," the doc demanded.

In a matter of moments, Doc Matlock had their new baby wrapped in a clean towel and lay her on her mother's chest. "Meet your new daughter, mom and dad," he said with a grin, continuing with his work.

Glen sat on the side of the bed, snuggled into his wife, and stared down at his new daughter. "I love you both so much," he said.

He thanked God for the day he met Eleanor, and prayed for a long and happy life together.

The End

From the Author

Thank you so much for reading my book – I hope you enjoyed it.

I would greatly appreciate you leaving a review on Amazon, even if it is only a one-liner. It helps to have my books more visible on Amazon!

About the Author

Multi-published, award-winning and bestselling author Cheryl Wright, former secretary, debt collector, account manager, writing coach, and shopping tour hostess, loves reading.

She writes both historical and contemporary western romance, as well as romantic suspense.

She lives in Melbourne, Australia, and is married with two adult children and has six grandchildren. When she's not writing, she can be found in her craft room making greeting cards.

Links:

Amazon Author Page:
https://www.amazon.com/author/cherylwright

Website: *http://www.cheryl-wright.com/*

Blog: *http://romance-authors.com/*

Facebook Reader Group:
https://www.facebook.com/groups/cherylwrightauth
or/